This book is to be returned on or before
the last date stamped below.

WITHDRAWN

This **Picture Mammoth** *belongs to*

_____

_____

a stitch in rhyme

Nursery Rhymes
with embroideries by
Belinda Downes

Contents

Jack and Jill

Jack and Jill went up the hill
To fetch a pail of water;
Jack fell down and broke his crown,
And Jill came tumbling after.

Then up Jack got and home did trot
As fast as he could caper;
And went to bed to mend his head
With vinegar and brown paper.

This Little Piggy

This little piggy went to market;

This little piggy stayed at home;

This little piggy had roast beef;

And this little piggy had none;

And this little piggy cried,
"Wee, wee, wee!"
All the way home.

There Was An Old Woman

There was an old woman tossed up in a basket
Seventeen times as high as the moon;
Where she was going, I couldn't but ask it,
For in her hand she carried a broom.

"Old woman, old woman, old woman," quoth I,
"O whither, O whither, O whither, so high?"
"To sweep the cobwebs from the sky!"
"Shall I go with thee?"
"Aye, by-and-by."

Polly, Put The Kettle On

Polly, put the kettle on,
Polly, put the kettle on,
Polly, put the kettle on,
We'll all have tea.

Sukey, take it off again,
Sukey, take it off again,
Sukey, take it off again,
They've all gone away.

Pussycat, Pussycat

Pussycat, pussycat, where have you been?
I've been to London to visit the Queen.
Pussycat, pussycat, what did you there?
I frightened a little mouse under the chair.

Little Bo-Peep

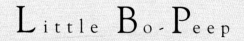

Little Bo-Peep has lost her sheep,
And can't tell where to find them;
Leave them alone, and they'll come home,
And bring their tails behind them.

Little Bo-Peep fell fast asleep,
And dreamed she heard them bleating;
But when she awoke she found it a joke,
For they were still a-fleeting.

Then up she took her little crook,
Determined for to find them;
She found them indeed, but it made her heart bleed,
For they'd left their tails behind them.

Mary, Mary, Quite Contrary

Mary, Mary, quite contrary,
How does your garden grow?
With silver bells and cockleshells,
And pretty maids all in a row.

I Love Little Pussy

I love little pussy, her coat is so warm:
And if I don't hurt her she'll do me no harm.
So I won't pull her tail nor drive her away,
But pussy and I very gently will play.

The Grand Old Duke Of York

Oh, the grand old Duke of York,
He had ten thousand men;
He marched them up to the top of the hill,
And he marched them down again.
And when they were up, they were up,
And when they were down, they were down,
And when they were only halfway up,
They were neither up nor down.

Hey, Diddle, Diddle

Hey, diddle, diddle!
The cat and the fiddle,
The cow jumped over the moon;
The little dog laughed
To see such sport,
And the dish ran away with the spoon.

Little Tommy Tittlemouse

Little Tommy Tittlemouse
Lived in a little house;
He caught fishes
In other men's ditches.

Monday's Child

Monday's child is fair of face,
Tuesday's child is full of grace,
Wednesday's child is full of woe,
Thursday's child has far to go,
Friday's child is loving and giving,
Saturday's child works hard for
a living.
But the child that is born on
the Sabbath day
Is blithe and bonny,
good and gay.

One, Two, Buckle My Shoe

One, two,
Buckle my shoe;

Three, four,
Knock at the door;

Five, six,
Pick up sticks;

Seven, eight,
Lay them straight;

Nine, ten,
A good fat hen.

Eleven, twelve,
Dig and delve;

Thirteen, fourteen,
Maids a-courting;

Fifteen, sixteen,
Maids in the kitchen;

Seventeen, eighteen,
Maids a-waiting;

Nineteen, twenty,
My plate's empty.

Sing A Song Of Sixpence

Sing a song of sixpence,
A pocket full of rye;
Four and twenty blackbirds
Baked in a pie.

When the pie was opened,
The birds began to sing;
Was not that a dainty dish
To set before the king?

The king was in his counting house
Counting out his money;
The queen was in the parlor
Eating bread and honey;

The maid was in the garden
Hanging out the clothes;
There came a little blackbird
And pecked off her nose.

Old King Cole

Old King Cole
Was a merry old soul,
And a merry old soul was he;
He called for his pipe,
And he called for his bowl,
And he called for his fiddlers three.

Now every fiddler, he had a fiddle,
And a very fine fiddle had he;
Oh, there's none so rare
As can compare
With King Cole and his
fiddlers three!

Little Miss Muffet

Little Miss Muffet
Sat on a tuffet,
Eating her curds and whey;
There came a great spider,
Who sat down beside her,
And frightened Miss Muffet away.

Jack Sprat

Jack Sprat could eat no fat,
His wife could eat no lean,
And so between them both, you see,
They licked the platter clean.

Humpty Dumpty

Humpty Dumpty sat on a wall,
Humpty Dumpty had a great fall;
All the King's horses, and all the King's men,
Couldn't put Humpty together again.

Hickory, Dickory, Dock

Hickory, dickory, dock!
The mouse ran up the clock;
The clock struck one,
The mouse ran down;
Hickory, dickory, dock!

Georgie Porgie

Georgie Porgie, pudding and pie,
Kissed the girls and made them cry;

When the boys came out to play,
Georgie Porgie ran away.

DOCTOR FOSTER

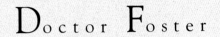

Doctor Foster went to Gloucester
In a shower of rain;
He stepped in a puddle,
Right up to his middle,
And never went there again.

HICKETY, PICKETY

Hickety, pickety, my black hen,
She lays eggs for gentlemen;
Sometimes nine, and sometimes ten,
Hickety, pickety, my black hen.

Ride A Cockhorse

Ride a cockhorse to Banbury Cross,
To see a fine lady upon a white horse;
With rings on her fingers and bells on her toes,
She shall have music wherever she goes.

Yankee Doodle

Yankee Doodle came to town,
Riding on a pony;
He stuck a feather in his cap
And called it macaroni.

Tommy Snooks

As Tommy Snooks and Bessy Brooks
Were walking out one Sunday,
Says Tommy Snooks to Bessy Brooks,
"Tomorrow will be Monday."

Old Mother Hubbard

Old Mother Hubbard
Went to the cupboard
To get her poor dog a bone;
But when she got there
The cupboard was bare,
And so the poor dog had none.

She went to the baker's
To buy him some bread;
But when she came back
The poor dog was dead.

She went to the undertaker's
To buy him a coffin;
But when she came back
The poor dog was laughing.

She took a clean dish
To get him some tripe;
But when she came back
He was smoking a pipe.

She went to the fishmonger's
To buy him some fish;
But when she came back
He was washing the dish.

She went to the hatter's
To buy him a hat;
But when she came back
He was feeding the cat.

She went to the barber's
To buy him a wig;
But when she came back
He was dancing a jig.

She went to the fruiterer's
To buy him some fruit;
But when she came back
He was playing the flute.

She went to the cobbler's
To buy him some shoes;
But when she came back
He was reading the news.

She went to the hosier's
To buy him some hose;
But when she came back
He was dressed in his clothes.

The dame made a curtsy,
The dog made a bow;
The dame said, "Your servant,"
The dog said, "Bow-wow."

Diddle, Diddle, Dumpling

Diddle, diddle, dumpling, my son John
Went to bed with his stockings on;
One shoe off and one shoe on,
Diddle, diddle, dumpling, my son John.

Hot Cross Buns!

Hot cross buns!
Old woman runs!
One a penny, two a penny,
Hot cross buns!

If you have no daughters,
Give them to your sons.
One a penny, two a penny,
Hot cross buns!

The Queen Of Hearts

The Queen of Hearts,
She made some tarts,
All on a summer's day;
The Knave of Hearts,
He stole those tarts,
And took them clean away.

The King of Hearts
Called for the tarts,
And beat the Knave full sore;
The Knave of Hearts
Brought back the tarts,
And vowed he'd steal no more.

Rub-a-dub-dub

Rub-a-dub-dub,
Three men in a tub;
And who do you think they be?
The butcher, the baker,
The candlestick-maker,
Turn 'em out, knaves all three.

Curly Locks! Curly Locks!

Curly Locks! Curly Locks! Will you be mine?
You shall not wash dishes, nor yet feed the swine,
But sit on a cushion and sew a fine seam,
And feed upon strawberries, sugar, and cream.

Wee Willie Winkie

Wee Willie Winkie runs through the town,
Upstairs and downstairs in his nightgown,
Rapping at the window, crying through the lock,
"Are the children in their beds,
for now it's eight o'clock?"

I Had A Little Nut Tree

I had a little nut tree,
Nothing would it bear
But a silver nutmeg
And a golden pear;
The King of Spain's daughter
Came to visit me,
And all for the sake
Of my little nut tree.
I skipped over water,
I danced over sea,
And all the birds in the air
Couldn't catch me.

One, Two, Three, Four, Five!

One, two, three, four, five!
I caught a fish alive.
Six, seven, eight, nine, ten!
I let it go again.
Why did you let it go?
Because it bit my finger so.
Which finger did it bite?
This little finger on the right.

Bobby Shaftoe

Bobby Shaftoe's gone to sea,
Silver buckles at his knee;
He'll come home and marry me,
Bonny Bobby Shaftoe.

Three Wise Men Of Gotham

Three wise men of Gotham
Went to sea in a bowl;
If the bowl had been stronger,
My story would have been longer.

Little Boy Blue

Little Boy Blue,
Come blow your horn,
The sheep's in the meadow,
The cow's in the corn.

Where is the boy
Who looks after the sheep?
He's under a haystack,
Fast asleep.

Will you wake him?
No, not I,
For if I do,
He's sure to cry.

Mother Goose

Old Mother Goose,
When she wanted to wander,
Would ride through the air
On a very fine gander.

And Old Mother Goose
The goose saddled soon,
And mounting its back,
Flew up to the moon.

The North Wind Doth Blow

The north wind doth blow,
And we shall have snow,
And what will poor Robin do then?
Poor thing.

He'll sit in a barn,
And keep himself warm,
And hide his head under his wing.
Poor thing.

If All The World Was Apple Pie

If all the world was apple pie,
And all the sea was ink,
And all the trees were bread and cheese,
What should we have to drink?

Where Are You Going To, My Pretty Maid?

"Where are you going to, my pretty maid?"
"I'm going a-milking, sir," she said.

"May I go with you, my pretty maid?"
"You're kindly welcome, sir," she said.

"What is your father, my pretty maid?"
"My father's a farmer, sir," she said.

"What is your fortune, my pretty maid?"
"My face is my fortune, sir," she said.

"Then I can't marry you, my pretty maid!"
"Nobody asked you, sir," she said.

Wᴴᴬᵀ Aʀᴇ Lɪᴛᴛʟᴇ Bᴏʏꜱ Mᴀᴅᴇ Oꜰ?

What are little boys made of, made of?
What are little boys made of?
"Frogs and snails and puppy dogs' tails,
That's what little boys are made of, made of."

What are little girls made of, made of?
What are little girls made of?
"Sugar and spice and all things nice,
That's what little girls are made of, made of."

MARY HAD A LITTLE LAMB

Mary had a little lamb,
With fleece as white as snow;
And everywhere that Mary went
The lamb was sure to go.

It followed her to school one day,
Which was against the rule;
It made the children laugh and play
To see a lamb at school.

There Was A Little Girl

There was a little girl, and she had a little curl
Right in the middle of her forehead;
When she was good, she was very, very good,
But when she was bad, she was horrid.

Hark, Hark, The Dogs Do Bark

Hark, hark, the dogs do bark,
The beggars are coming to town:
Some in rags, and some in jags,
And one in a velvet gown.

Little Jack Horner

Little Jack Horner,
Sat in the corner,
Eating a Christmas pie;
He put in his thumb,
And pulled out a plum,
And said, "What a good boy am I."

Ladybird, Ladybird

Ladybird, ladybird, fly away home
Your house is on fire, your children are gone —
All but one, and her name is Ann,
And she crept under the pudding pan.

Ring-a-Ring o' Roses

Ring-a-ring o' roses
A pocket full of posies,
A-tishoo! A-tishoo!
We all fall down.

The cows are in the meadow,
Lying fast asleep.
A-tishoo! A-tishoo!
We all get up again.

First published in Great Britain 1996
by Methuen Children's Books
Published 1997 by Mammoth
an imprint of Reed International Books Limited
Michelin House, 81 Fulham Road, London, SW3 6RB
and Auckland and Melbourne

10 9 8 7 6 5 4 3 2 1

ISBN 0 7497 3022 6

A CIP catalogue record for this title
is available from the British Library

Produced by Mandarin Offset Ltd
Printed and bound in China